For Martin and Katy with love   KW

For Esme BW

Text copyright © Karen Wallace 1997
Illustrations copyright © Bee Willey 1997

First published in Great Britain in 1997
by Hodder Children's Books

10 9 8 7 6 5 4 3 2 1

ISBN 0 340 66086 4 (HB)
0 340 66087 2 (PB)

Printed in Singapore

Hodder Children's Books
a division of Hodder Headline plc
338 Euston Road, London NW1 3BH

Blue Eyes

Karen Wallace
and
BeeWilley

Hodder
Children's
Books

a division of Hodder Headline plc

I am in a field looking for treasure.
I don't know what I'll find.
A glass bottle or a seashell, a bone or a feather.
The field looks like a brown sea around me.
I shade my eyes and search like a sailor.
Something glitters in the sun.
It is a brooch made of silver.

A deer, a rabbit, a lion and an eagle are locked in a circle.
Their eyes are blue stones.
They are the bluest blue I have ever seen.
I run all the way home.
My grandmother is sitting in her chair.
She holds my brooch and tells me this story.

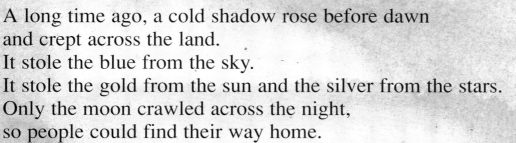

A long time ago, a cold shadow rose before dawn
and crept across the land.
It stole the blue from the sky.
It stole the gold from the sun and the silver from the stars.
Only the moon crawled across the night,
so people could find their way home.

At that time there was a waterfall hidden in the forest.
A girl stood on a ledge behind the water.
Her skin was white as ice.
Her hair was silver and fell to her shoulders.
Her eyes were blue like the bluest sky.
The girl was hiding in the waterfall.
She was hiding from the cold shadow
who wanted to steal the blue from her eyes,
so the land would become a grey place, forever.
The silver girl cried for help.
But her tears only made the waterfall louder.

One day a deer climbed up the slippery rocks
to eat a patch of grass.
She saw two blue eyes sparkling behind the water.
'Find me my brother,' cried the silver girl. 'He is
hiding in another shape so the shadow
cannot find him.'
'Then how could *I* ever find him?' asked the deer.
'Because his eyes are blue like mine,' said the girl.
'Bring him to me and we can drive the cold shadow
from the land.'
'I will do my best,' said the deer.
'It is our only chance,' said the silver girl.
      'And in return I promise you,
            and anyone who helps you,
                  eyes as blue as mine,
                        forever.'

The deer climbed down the side of the waterfall
into the meadow. A rabbit was nibbling a
buttercup in the long grass.
Suddenly a lion leapt from the forest.
He grabbed the deer by the neck and dragged
her to the ground.
His teeth pressed like nails against her skin.
'Don't kill me!' cried the deer and she told
the lion about the silver girl.
But the lion didn't care about the silver girl.
He was hungry and the deer was plump.
'Remember,' said the deer, 'if you help me,
you will have eyes as blue as the bluest sky,
forever.'

The lion thought again.
A lion with blue eyes would be the
most frightening lion in the land.
He opened his jaws and let the deer go.
'I have seen such a blue,' he said. 'High on the mountain.'

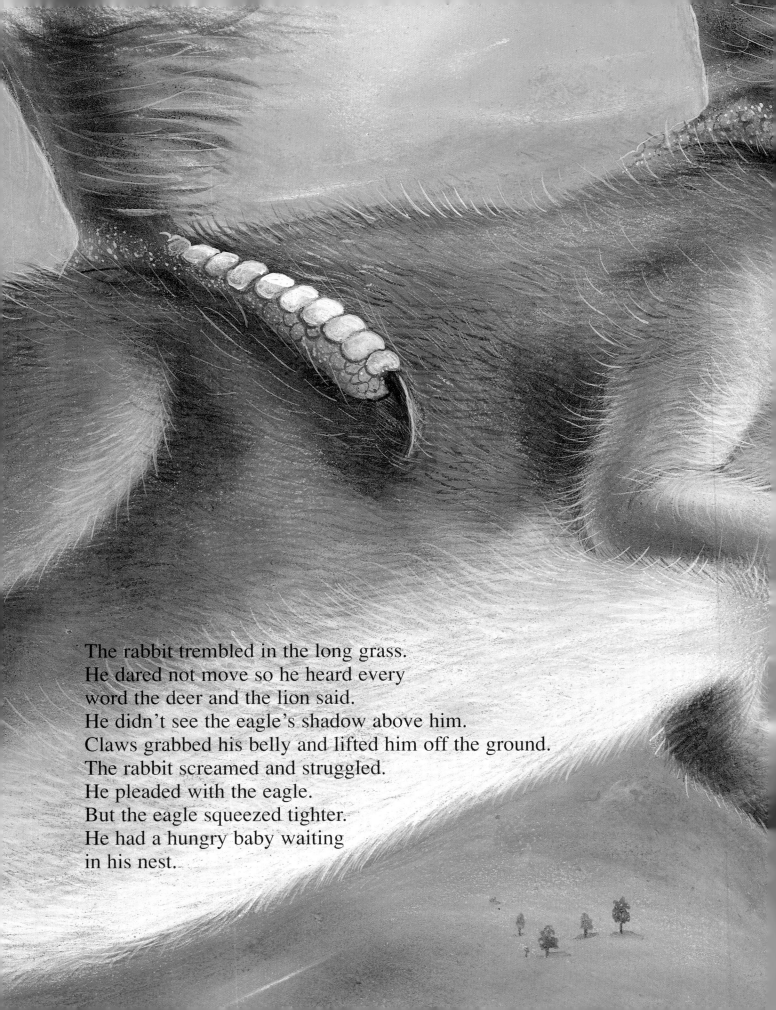

The rabbit trembled in the long grass.
He dared not move so he heard every
word the deer and the lion said.
He didn't see the eagle's shadow above him.
Claws grabbed his belly and lifted him off the ground.
The rabbit screamed and struggled.
He pleaded with the eagle.
But the eagle squeezed tighter.
He had a hungry baby waiting
in his nest.

Far below, the rabbit saw the deer and the lion
climbing the mountain.
He struggled one more time.
The eagle landed on a branch. His curved beak
plunged towards the rabbit's belly.
'Don't kill me!' cried the rabbit.
He told the eagle about the silver girl.
The eagle looked down at the lion and deer.
An eagle with blue eyes would be the
most frightening eagle in the land, he thought.
He picked up the rabbit and carried him to the mountain.

The lion and the deer were resting
by the edge of a lake.
'We must wait here,' said the eagle.
'I have seen such a blue by this lake.'
The animals waited but they saw nothing.
The water in the lake was black and still.
The cliffs were steep and rocky.
The rabbit looked at the deer.
It was a lonely place to be.
Soon the lion grew restless.
He laid his heavy paw on the deer's neck.
The eagle put his claw over the rabbit's tail.
'If you eat us now,' said the deer, 'your eyes
will never be blue and the cold shadow will
swallow the land.'
'Who cares about blue eyes if you have to
go hungry?' growled the lion.

Suddenly a huge fish leapt out of the lake.
His scales were white.
His fins were silver.
His eyes were blue like the bluest sky.
They were blue as the eyes of the silver girl.
'We have found the one we were looking for,'
said the deer.
'We must hurry before the cold shadow
finds him too,' said the rabbit.

The huge fish leapt again.
This time the eagle caught him and
held him gently as he could.
And all the way down the mountain, the lion
carried the silver fish like a precious cub in his jaws.

But when they reached the waterfall, the lion could not
climb to the ledge where the silver girl was hiding.
The rocks were too slippery.
The silver fish gasped and flapped in his jaws.
'He is dying,' screamed the eagle. 'Drop him in the pool!'
The huge fish turned upside down.
Then he sank.
Water poured down the rocks into the pool.
The silver girl was crying, crying harder than
she had ever cried before.
Above them, the cold shadow blotted out the
mountain and crept towards the forest.
'We did our best,' said the deer. 'Each one of us
in our own way. Now there is nothing else we can do.'
The lion and the eagle would have cried, if they could.
At that moment, the huge fish leapt out of the pool.
His eyes were stars above the spray.
He landed on the ledge.

He became the brother the silver girl
had been waiting for.
As they stood together, a blue light
blazed through the water.
It danced in the air and sparkled
over the forest.
The silver girl and her brother
stepped from the waterfall.
Their eyes were blue like the bluest sky.
Above them, the sky was blue again.
A fiery sun rolled from behind a cloud.
The cold shadow faded from the mountain
and fled like a ghost from the land.

'Look,' whispered the deer. 'She has kept her promise.'
A brooch glittered at the silver girl's shoulder.
A deer, a rabbit, a lion and an eagle were locked in a circle.
Their eyes were blue stones.
They were blue like the bluest sky.

My grandmother hands me back my brooch.
I look at the deer, the rabbit, the lion and the eagle.
I know their eyes will be blue, forever.